T(

Morgan's Secret

FIRST NOVELS

The New Series

Formac Publishing Company Limited
Haifax, Nova Scotia

Formac Publishing Company Limited acknowledges the support of the Cultural Affairs Section, Nova Scotia Department of Tourism and Culture. We acknowledge the financial support of the Government of Canada through the Book Publishing Industry Development Program (BPIDP) for our publishing activities. We acknowledge the support of the Canada Council for the Arts for our publishing program.

Canadian Cataloguing in Publication Data

Staunton, Ted, 1956-

Morgan's secret

    (First Novels. The new series)
    ISBN 0-88780-494-2 (pbk)

    ISBN 0-88780-495-0 (bound)

I. Slavin, Bill. II. Title. III. Series.

PS8587.T334M68   2000   jC813'.54   C99-950275-1
PZ7.S8076Mo 2000

Formac Publishing
Company Limited
5502 Atlantic Street
Halifax, NS B3H 1G4

Distributed in the U.S. by
Orca Book Publishers
P.O. Box 468 Custer, WA
U.S.A. 98240-0468

Printed and bound in Canada.

Table of Contents

1
Sports, food, and secrets

It's a gym day. I like gym, but mostly because it comes right before lunch. I'm crummy at sports but I'm great at eating. I'm pretty good at talking too.

Today Mrs. Ross has us outside for soccer-baseball. I'm not sure exactly, but my team is either winning or losing. It's hard to remember with lunch so close. Besides, the most exciting thing that's happened so far has been Aldeen Hummel stealing second base. Not sliding stealing, *stealing* stealing. For

a long time she ran around
with it in the outfield. Aldeen
is the Godzilla of Grade Three.
She does stuff like that.

I do know it's our ups. That's why I'm sitting here on the bench, kicking dust and wondering what I've got for dessert. Now everybody's shouting. I look up as my best friend Charlie blasts across home plate. Charlie's good at sports.

Everybody cheers; I clap too. Charlie plops down beside me, all red in the face.

"Did you see it?" he asks.

"What?" I say. "Did you get a homer?"

Charlie rolls his eyes. "Erin's kick! She booted one way over Ben's head. I was on second. Now she's on third."

I look over to third base. Erin is standing there, pushing

her black curls behind her ears. I feel Charlie lean in close.

"Know what?" he whispers. "I really like her."

Before I can say anything, everyone is calling me.

"Hurry, Morgan!"

"You're up! Get Erin home and we win!"

I jog over to the plate like I'm Mark McGwire or somebody. Soccer-baseball is simple. The teacher rolls the ball, you hoof it and run. Mrs. Ross rolls and WHAMMO! I connect. The ball takes off like a rocket — right at Aldeen Hummel. It whomps into her stomach and she holds on for the catch. I'm out. She grins as if she's just eaten New York.

My team groans. The other team cheers. Aldeen won't give up the ball. Everything is back to normal. As we line up to go in, Charlie whispers to me: "Know what I said about Erin? Don't tell anybody, okay?"

Charlie looks worried. What does he think I am, a blabber-mouth or something?

2
Not quite perfect

Well, I'm not a blabbermouth;
I'm just not perfect, either. It
happened like this. Right after
lunch Mrs. Ross gave us
partners for science work. She
made me work with Aldeen
Hummel.

Aldeen makes me nervous.
She makes everybody nervous,
even grownups. And when I
get nervous, I talk. Aldeen
never says much, unless she's
yelling at somebody. So I was
blabbing away when all of a
sudden Aldeen said, "Do you
like girls?"

I was so surprised I shut up. Aldeen glared at me. Her witchy hair was sticking out like pointing fingers. I burped. "Well," I said, "Some."

If one of the guys had asked me, I'd have yelled "NO!" right off: that's what you'd have to do. But hey, Aldeen was a girl. I didn't like her a whole lot, but we'd helped each other one time, and there were some girls that were okay. Besides, I didn't want her to flatten me. I said, "But not to get married or anything."

Aldeen snorted. "I didn't ask *that*. That's gross. Anyway, you're wrong. Girls and boys hate each other."

"Do not."

"Do too."

"What about when — " I was going to say "when we helped each other?" but I chickened out. Aldeen glared at me some more. I got even more nervous. I looked around the room. Charlie was with Erin. He was all red in the face again. Before I even thought, I said,

"Okay, what about how Charlie really likes Erin, huh?"

Aldeen looked at them. I froze. What had I just said?

"But don't tell anybody," I said really fast, "It's a secret."

The Godzilla of Grade Three grinned as if she was about to crunch New York again. Now I think I might just be New York.

3
A rough ride

So now I have a secret — that I blabbed Charlie's secret.

After school, Charlie and I go bike riding down by the creek. Charlie's in the lead; I'm in trouble. Why, oh why, oh why, oh why can't I keep my big mouth shut? Aldeen is going to tell Charlie's secret to the whole world. In my mind I can see her on top of the monkey bars, in her purple sweatsuit, waving her arms and yelling. Charlie will get teased forever. He'll also know who to blame. He'll never speak to me again.

The path we're riding twists and turns through the bushes. I try to keep up, but all the time I'm thinking, *what can I do?* I've gotta do something about Hummel the Bummel. It's the only way I can keep my secret secret.

I could give her money. Except I don't have any right now. Besides, Aldeen would probably take the money and still tell.

I could beg her not to tell. Ha ha. Okay, skip that one.

I could trick her somehow. I don't know the somehow. My record for tricking people isn't too hot anyhow.

I could drop a piano on her head. Yeah, right. I imagine a piano breaking apart on Aldeen's witchy head and her not even noticing.

We whump across a big root on our bikes, then zoom down a drop so fast I get elevator stomach. "Whoah!" I yell. Charlie is laughing.

Maybe I could hide for a hundred years at the bottom of a deep, dark hole. I'd need a lot of snacks, though. And there'd be nobody to play with. Of course, after Aldeen gets finished screaming from the top of the climbers, I won't have a friend anyway: my hiding isn't going to help Charlie.

We do skids in the dirt to stop. "Cool," Charlie says. I nod. I'm huffing like a walrus. Maybe if Charlie talks about Erin again, I could find a way to warn him.

Instead, my friend says, "Let's go again. You first this time."

When I get home I'm going to start digging. I hate secrets.

4
Aldeen's army

My parents won't let me dig a hole. Next morning I hope I'm sick, but I'm not. Instead I shuffle off to doomsday with my lunch.

Only nothing happens. Well, not exactly nothing. Aldeen steps on everyone's feet as we line up for library. She accidentally-on-purpose knocks over the new-book shelf when we get there. Then she stays in the washroom for most of math. But that's all usual stuff. I mean nothing happens about the secret.

Then the recess bell goes and everything changes. I'm lining up for outside when Aldeen butts in behind me. She jabs me low in the back with her bony old finger. There's a lot of me there, and it hurts.

"Ow!" I jump and whip around. Aldeen is holding a raggedy tennis ball.

"You hafta play with me today," she says.

"What?" I say.

"You heard me," she says. Her eyes get all narrow behind her smudgy glasses. "'Cause if you don't, I'll tell."

The line starts moving. Forget my snack, my stomach feels like that hole I was going to dig, only filled with

monsters. When we get
outside, Ben calls, "Ghost
tag. Count potatoes for it."
Everybody sticks out fists.

"I can't play," I tell them,
and take off before they ask
why. "I'll play at lunch."

Aldeen is waiting over on the pavement.

"Wallball," she orders like an army general, "I'll win. We'll play at lunch, too."

5
The unfriendly friend

It's been three days of bossing by Hummel the Bummel, Queen Aldeen the Mean. I don't have time to play with anyone but her, not even Charlie. We play before school, after school, lunch, and recess. We play wallball, tag, hopscotch, tetherball; we play foursquare with just two people, and Aldeen always wins.

Partly she wins because she rockets around about a million miles an hour. Partly she wins because I stink at games.

Mostly she wins because she cheats. Her shots are in even when they're out; mine are out even when they're in. She fudges the score; she changes the rules. She pushes, elbows, trips, swats and pounds. And every time I say anything her eyes go all squinchy and she says, "You don't want me to tell, do you?"

Today she wants me to stay after school again.

"I can't," I lie, "I've gotta go out with my mom." Really I'm biking with Charlie.

Queen Aldeen gets that squinchy look and I turn into Morgan the Chicken Boy again.

"I'll be outside," she says happily. On the way, she trips Mark just for fun.

I go to Charlie. "I gotta do something first," I tell him.

"Like what," he says, "Play with Aldeen?" It's the first time he's said anything about me playing with her. Charlie never talks much.

I don't know what to say. I shrug. My shoulder hurts where Aldeen elbowed me at recess.

"I'll be at the creek," Charlie says. He walks off fast.

Aldeen is waiting at the doors, bouncing her raggedy tennis ball.

"Foursquare," she says. "I start."

She makes me play until everyone's gone home. The door of the school opens and out comes Mrs. Ross.

"Still here?" she smiles. "You two are playing a lot these days."

I rub my side where Aldeen has just whacked me. Aldeen slaps a dirty band-aid back across her knee.

"That's right," she says, "We're friends."

I start running.

6
Heart-thumping
tongue tripper

At home I stuff as many cookies as I can into my mouth and ride like crazy for the creek. Charlie is down at the end of the path.

"Made it," I pant.

"Come on," Charlie says.

We ride the path up and down, maybe five times. We go so fast, I can't tell which rattles more, my bike chain or my teeth. By the time we stop I'm almost eating my cookies again. We straddle our bikes and watch the creek trickle by.

"Are you still mad?" I ask Charlie.

He shrugs. "How come we don't play any more?"

I pretend I don't know what he means. "We're playing now."

"Well, how come you play with her? Everybody says she's like your — "

"SHE IS NOT!"

Girlfriends! Charlie should talk, boy. I guess he knows it too, because his face is red. I say, "I can't tell; it's secret. But if you knew, you'd thank me."

I like that. It makes me sound noble and brave. I want to make it sound even better. I whisper, "See, Aldeen found out this secret about me? And unless I play with her she's going to blab it from the top of the monkey bars."

"Wow. What's the secret?"

Uh-oh. I haven't figured that out yet.

"C'mon," Charlie says, "I told you mine." His face is even redder.

I say, "Well, Aldeen said boys hate girls so I said no and she said yes, so I said —"

A real whopper has just popped into my head. I'm going to say I like Diane Gruber, this girl in our class. Charlie is all ears. He's leaning forward. My heart is thumping so hard it trips my tongue. "— so I said no, because you liked Diane Gruber, no, I

mean you liked Erin, NO! I mean *I* liked —"

"You told." Charlie's face has gone from red to white.

"No!" I shout, "I said —"

"You liar, Morgan." Charlie is already wheeling his bike around, "You *told*."

"But now I'm —"

"Liar." Charlie burns off up the path. I don't go after him. Even if I caught him what would I say — that he's right?

7
Swing shift

Aldeen is waiting on the swings next morning.

"You gotta push me," she says.

Who cares now? I'd like to push her into the next galaxy.

"Get lost, Aldeen."

She blinks. Then she mashes her lips flat together. "If you don't …"

"Go tell. See if I care."

For a second she looks almost disappointed. Then she hops off the swing.

"You're dead," she says. She starts to march away.

"Thanks a bunch, Aldeen," I call after her. "Guess that's why you said we were friends."

"Not any more," she calls back.

"Ha ha. Guess what? We never were. Friends don't do stuff like you do."

She wheels around. "Oh yeah? What do friends do?" She makes it sound like a word for babies.

I don't care. I say, "They play with each other. They —"

"We play with each other."

"That's because you make me. Real friends play together because they like to."

"Well," Aldeen says, "I —" She stops.

I barely notice, I'm so mad. I say, "Real friends

don't say they'll blab secrets."

Aldeen says, "You blabbed Charlie's secret."

Now I stop. "Well," I lie, "he doesn't care. Real friends don't care if you do bad stuff by mistake. They forgive you. Know that word, Aldeen? For-give?"

"Well, that's stupid," says Aldeen.

"It is not," I practically shout, "It's smart. And friends listen to you, too. And do stuff that you want to do sometimes. And they share stuff, Aldeen. And they don't cheat. Not like you!"

Aldeen stares at me. Then she says, "Well that sucks. It's stupid. Forget it. I'll think I'll just blab Charlie's big fat secret instead." She twists away on her popsicle stick legs and she's gone.

Luke and Ian walk by. "Lovers' quarrel?" they say and go off snickering.

I swat at the swing chain and hurt my hand. Things have gone from bad to worse to whatever comes next all at once. I sure hope Charlie forgives me. If he doesn't, I'm going to be mad at him, too.

8
Playing keepaway

Charlie keeps away; he does not forgive me. So now I'm mad at everyone and everyone is mad at me — or laughing and making kissy faces. All day long I watch Aldeen, then Charlie. Charlie watches Aldeen, then me. Aldeen doesn't watch anybody. It's like we're invisible. The way everybody else is giggling about me, I wish I were.

All morning I wait for Aldeen to blab Charlie's secret. At recess she tries to climb the flagpole. I figure she's heading up to yell to everyone. I bet Charlie thinks the same thing, because he freezes. She gets a little way up, slips, and kicks Phil in the head. A teacher comes over to get her down. Aldeen yells a lot of stuff, but nothing about Charlie. I'm glad, I think.

At lunch I sit by myself. I hardly eat anything, for me: I don't even finish my second sandwich. There's a crash at the back of the lunchroom. I turn. Aldeen is writing STUPID CHAR on the blackboard in pink chalk. I stop chewing.

STUPID CHARE, she finishes. I see she's broken her chair. Aldeen is not a good speller.

By the end of afternoon recess she still hasn't said anything. I don't get it, but right now I don't care. Things haven't been this bad since I first moved here. I'm so alone I almost miss playing with Aldeen.

Almost. Playing with Aldeen was weird. You never knew what was going to happen next. Well, yeah, you did — she was going to get you — but I mean, you never knew how she was going to do it. It was kind of exciting; different from playing with Charlie, that's for sure. And hey, who else could have played with Aldeen and survived? Pretty cool, eh? I feel myself puff up a little, then I remember now and shrink way back down. Compared with now, those days were practically fun.

9
Marshmallow moment

After school Aldeen marches off, her shoelaces flapping. Charlie leaves with Dylan and Josh. I go home alone.

Charlie and Aldeen, I huff to myself. What did Charlie have to go and tell me a secret for? It's all his fault. And Aldeen's. If she weren't Hummel the Bummel I wouldn't have gotten all nervous and blabbed. Even if I had, no one but her would have done this.

When I get home I sneak a bag of marshmallows out to

the back yard. Up in my play-fort I eat one, then squeeze a couple in my fist. I want to keep on feeling mad. It's better than feeling like a marsh-mallow.

I open my fist. The marsh-mallows puff back out a little. I sigh. Okay, so it was my fault, too. I didn't have to blab. But if Charlie is my friend, isn't he supposed to forgive me? I mean, look how hard I've tried to make up for it. Or is it that, if I'm Charlie's friend, I'm supposed to forgive him for not forgiving me for messing up? Would that mean that we're still friends? How would I know?

My brain is starting to feel like, well, marshmallows. I

eat the ones in my hand. Eating usually helps me think. Do I still want to be friends with Charlie? Yeah. How can I show him? I can't steal his secret back. But, but, BUT: I can look just as dumb!

I swallow. I know what I have to do. Just knowing makes me feel good enough to have a few more marshmallows. I climb out of the playfort and go in to call Charlie. I hope he's there; I have to do this before I chicken out. On the way I have another marshmallow.

10
A bounce in the middle

Charlie doesn't exactly jump for joy, but he says okay. Except he won't tell Aldeen. I don't want to either, so I write her a note instead. It says: *Here is another secret Morgan likes Diane.*

I race in before school and leave it on Aldeen's new chair. Charlie watches her find it when she comes in. Now if Aldeen blabs, at least we'll both be in for it.

The only thing is, she *still* doesn't say anything. Charlie and I watch her at recess. We

don't feel much like playing.
Aldeen just sits by herself,
picking at her scabby knees.
She doesn't even bug anybody.

The whole day goes by with
us worried and Aldeen not
talking. And the next, and the
next. It's hard to tell which is
worse: getting teased forever or
waiting to get teased forever.

"Why is she doing this to
us?" Charlie wonders as we
walk home.

"Because she's Aldeen the
Mean," I say. "One time when
I had to play with her she told
Mrs. Ross we were friends.
What a joke. I bet she never
had a friend in her whole
life. I'm never gonna forgive
her for this, boy."

Next morning when I go into class there's a blue ball on my desk. It's not mine. "This yours?" I ask the kids at the desks around mine. They say no. I'm not sure how it got there. I know that sometimes the caretaker leaves stuff on desks if he finds it when he's sweeping up. Maybe that's what happened.

Anyway it's a good ball, and I'm tired of worrying about things. At recess I take it outside and show it to Charlie. He gives it a test bounce.

"Cool," he says.

"Wanta play something?" I ask. "It's better than waiting for Aldeen to blab on us."

Charlie nods and throws it off the wall; I catch it on the bounce. I'm winding up to throw back when Charlie says, "Oh-oh."

I turn and — oh no, this is it. There she is — Aldeen Hummel is steaming towards us.

"Hey" she's yelling "That's my ball!"

And all at once I understand. Aldeen left the ball on my desk just to get us to try and have fun so she could wreck it. I bet all along she's just been waiting for us to look happy. What a dirty trick.

She huffs up in front of us, the Godzilla of Grade Three, witchy hair bouncing, band-aids flapping, shoelaces flopping in the dust. I can almost smell smoke coming out of her ears.

She lifts her bony finger and points. I see Charlie's face go red. I shut my eyes for her shout.

It doesn't come. Nothing happens.

"Hey Bozo," I hear her say impatiently. I open my eyes. Now I see she's not pointing at us. She's pointing at the ball.

"That's mine," she says again, only quieter. And then, almost as if she's shy or something Aldeen Hummel says, "... but I'll forgive you."

Four more new novels in the New First Novels Series:

Duff's Monkey Business
by Budge Wilson/ Illustrated by Kim LaFave
Duff is known for his vivid imagination. So when Duff announces he has discovered a monkey in the family barn nobody believes him. Just when everyone has had enough of Duff's tall tales a circus comes to town minus its star monkey. Could Duff be telling the truth after all?

Jan on the Trail
Monica Hughes/ Illustrated by Carlos Freire
When Jan and Sarah learn that Patch, their beloved dog friend, has been lost, they decide to become detectives and find him. Following the trail isn't easy but the girls are resourceful. They set off to follow the clues with the hope of reuniting Patch with his new owner.

Lilly Plays her Part

By Brenda Bellingham/
Illustrated by Elizabeth Owen

Lilly is happy because she has been chosen to be Gretel in the school musical, *Hansel and Gretel.* She is really looking forward to the play until it becomes obvious to everyone that her best friend Minna has been miscast as the evil witch. They need someone to play the witch who can sing, act and cackle — Lilly! Lilly is very disappointed. She really wanted to be Gretel, not the evil witch. Lilly struggles with her new role until she discovers that playing a witch can be fun.

Robyn Looks For Bears

Hazel Hutchins/ Illustrated by Yvonne Cathcart

Robyn goes to her cousin's mountain tourist lodge near Bear Lake for the summer. She is determined to see a bear so she will have an exciting story to tell her city friends about her summer vacation. Robyn's quest for bears leads to lots of fun but no bears. Then when she least expects it her dreams come true.

Look for these New First Novels!

Meet Duff
Duff's Monkey Business
Duff the Giant Killer

Meet Jan
Jan on the Trail
Jan and Patch
Jan's Big Bang

Meet Lilly
Lilly's Good Deed
Lilly to the Rescue

Meet Robyn
Robyn Looks for Bears
Robyn's Want Ad
Shoot for the Moon, Robyn

Meet Morgan
Morgan's Secret
Morgan and the Money
Morgan Makes Magic

Meet Carrie
Carrie's Crowd
Go For It, Carrie

Meet all the great kids in the First Novels Series!

Meet Arthur
Arthur Throws a Tantrum
Arthur's Dad
Arthur's Problem Puppy

Meet Fred
Fred and the Flood
Fred and the Stinky Cheese
Fred's Dream Cat

Meet Leo
Leo and Julio

Meet the Loonies
Loonie Summer
The Loonies Arrive

Meet Maddie
Maddie Tries To Be Good
Maddie in Trouble
Maddie in Hospital
Maddie Goes to Paris
Maddie in Danger
Maddie in Goal
Maddie Wants Music
That's Enough Maddie!

Meet Marilou
Marilou on Stage

Meet Max
Max the Superhero

Meet Mikey
Mikey Mite's Best Present
Good For You, Mikey Mite!
Mikey Mite Goes to School
Mikey Mite's Big Problem

Meet Mooch
Missing Mooch
Mooch Forever
Hang On, Mooch!
Mooch Gets Jealous
Mooch and Me

Meet Raphael
Video Rivals

Meet the Swank Twins
The Swank Prank
Swank Talk

Meet Will
Will and His World

Formac Publishing Company Limited
5502 Atlantic Street, Halifax, Nova Scotia B3H 1G4
Orders: 1-800-565-1975 Fax: (902) 425-0166